'Roland Harvey's illustrations are full of humour, warmth and good fun and readers of all ages will delight in pouring over them – giggling and reminiscing as they turn each page.'
Good Reading

'This is a great picture book for readers of all ages.'
Magpies

'This book begs to be read again and again, not only to locate Roland's lost items, but to enjoy the detail and energy of the illustration. Highly recommended for all readers and younger children as well. A wonderfully idiosyncratic view of holiday life and the Australian way.'
Reading Time

———————————

Short-listed: Picture Book of the Year, Children's Book Council Awards, 2005

Short-listed: Best Designed Children's Picture Book, 53rd APA Book Design Awards, 2005

Short-listed: Book of the Year, Best Book for Language Development, Speech Pathology Australia, 2005

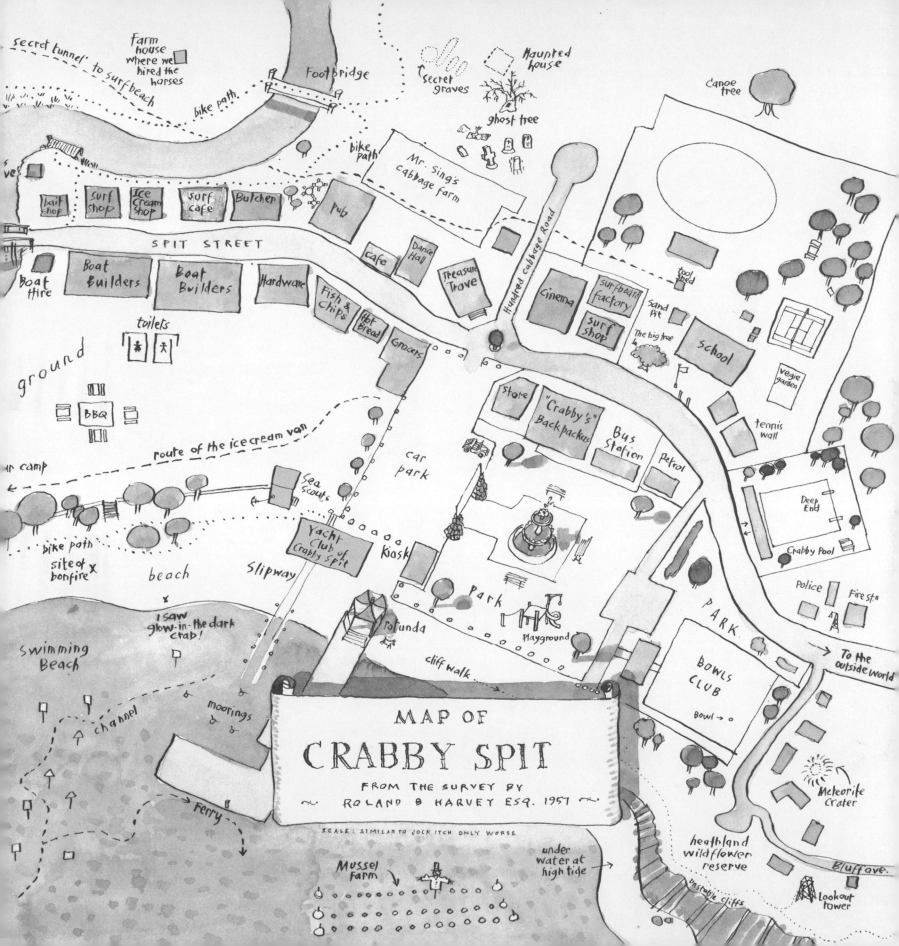

secret tunnel? to surf beach

Farm house where we hired the horses

Footbridge

secret graves

Haunted house

ghost tree

canoe tree

bike path

bike path

Mr. Sing's cabbage farm

bait shop

surf shop

Ice Cream shop

surf cafe

Butcher

pub

SPIT STREET

cafe

Dance Hall

Treasure Trove

Hundred Cabbage Road

Cinema

surfboard factory

tool shed

sand Pit

The big tree

surf shop

School

vegie garden

Boat Hire

Boat Builders

Boat Builders

Hardware

Fish & Chips

Hot Bread

Grocers

tennis wall

toilets

store

"Crabby's" Backpackers

Bus Station

Petrol

Deep End

ground

BBQ

route of the ice cream van

car park

Crabby Pool

ur camp

Sea Scouts

Police

Fire st.n

bike path

site of bonfire

beach

Slipway

Yacht Club of Crabby Spit

Kiosk

Park

Playground

PARK

To the outside World

Swimming Beach

I saw glow-in-the-dark crab!

Rotunda

cliff walk

BOWLS CLUB

Bowl →

channel

moorings

MAP OF

CRABBY SPIT

FROM THE SURVEY BY
ROLAND O HARVEY ESQ. 1957

SCALE: SIMILAR TO JOCK ITCH ONLY WORSE

Meteorite Crater

heathland wildflower reserve

Bluff ave.

Ferry

Mussel farm

under water at high tide

unstable cliffs

Lookout tower

First published in 2004
First paperback edition published in 2006

Allen & Unwin
83 Alexander St
Crows Nest NSW 2065
Australia
Phone: (61 2) 8425 0100
Fax: (61 2) 9906 2218
Email: info@allenandunwin.com
Web: www.allenandunwin.com

National Library of Australia
Cataloguing-in-Publication entry:

Harvey, Roland, 1945– .
At the beach : postcards from Crabby Spit.

Paperback ed.
For children.
ISBN 978 1 74114 704 9 (pbk).

1. Vacations – Juvenile fiction. I. Title.

A823.3

Illustration technique: dip pen and watercolour
Designed by Roland Harvey and by Sandra Nobes
Printed in China by Everbest Printing Co., Ltd

5 7 9 10 8 6 4

For Frankie

At the BEACH

Postcards from Crabby Spit

Roland Harvey

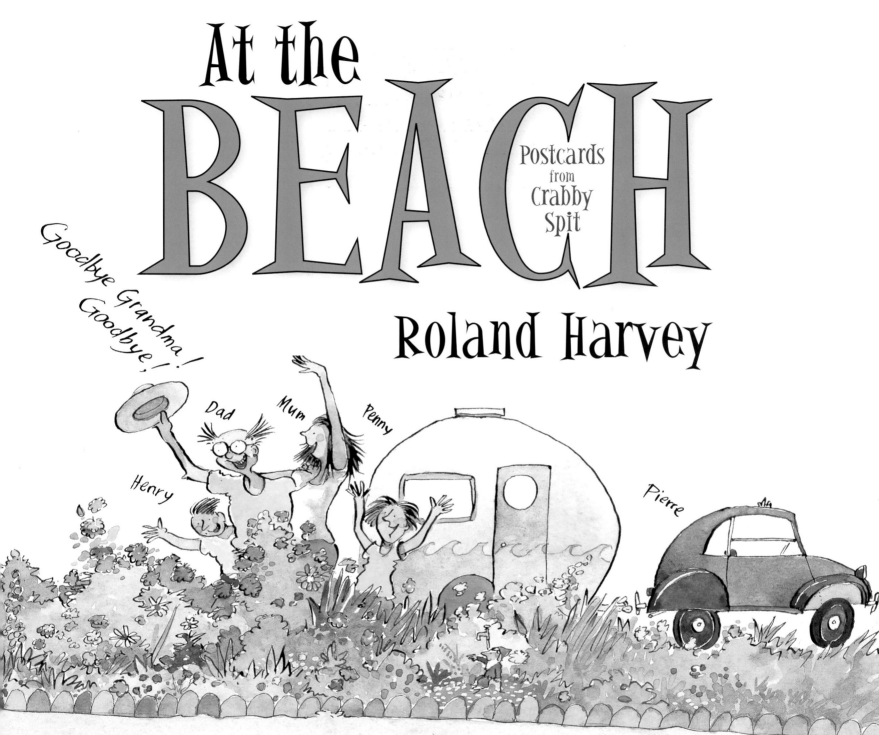

Goodbye Grandma! Goodbye!!

Henry · Dad · Mum · Penny · Pierre

ALLEN&UNWIN

Dear Grandma
We are nearly at Crabby Spit! On the way we had to stop 3 times and Frankie was sick 4 times. We saw a policeman and he told dad to speed up because he was holding up traffic.
We saw a monster in a lake and I saw 12 baby ducks and 2 giant crabs.
Rajah found a towel beside the road! I can't wait to get to Crabby Spit. I drew us for you. Love from Henry

Rajah   Dad   Mum   Penny   Henry   Frankie

Dear Grandma, Crabby Spit is COOL!
We have the best camping spot right near the
toilets and the beach and the river. Mum has
agreed to stop embarrassing us and only wear her
new hat in the tent if we do ALL the cooking for
the whole holiday. One family has brought their
mower and we are getting fish and chips for tea
and then going looking for crabs. There is a bike
track and a river and horse riding and mosquitoes.

Love from Henry

Dear Grandma ... WOW!! It's all happening at Crabby.
Dad says the lifesavers are wanting him to join the club
and Mr. Mac Intosh was chased by a shark. It must
have been scared off by the taste of his shorts. And I
saw a bird drop a poo on a kid's hand. I'm going to
join the lifesavers and row the surfboat and drive the
rubber duckies. I tell you what, Grandma, surfing is
ace. I am going to get really good and be world champ.
There was a hang-gliderer and I want to be worldchamp
of that too. That's after I get to be world champignon at
Frisbee. I drew this picture
of a hang-gliderer for you! ——————
♡ love ♡ Penny

Dear Grandma, We are having a good time here at Crabby Spit. At the Sand Sculpture Competition today Mrs. Thomas made Mr. Thomas into a mermaid and won! The kids helped dad build a sandcastle and Uncle Kevin is going to have another go at the surfboard. One kid thinks he is a seagull and a little dog did a wee on a lady's foot. Some people have been catching fish and they showed us how to clean them. I have become a vegetarian. I don't know how the seagull kid does it. He only stays up for about 20 seconds so I think he's cheating.

♡ Penny

Dear Grandma, I bet you would love Crabby Spit.
It is so windy today that I saw some underpants fly
across the camping ground. The last I saw they were
on the back of a lady's head.
We played Scrabble in the annexe and had hot chocolate
and marshmallow floaters. Afterwards we helped clean
up the beach. Mr Thomas' stuff floated away yesterday and
today the wind is blowing it all back again! Dad is going to
buy a heap of fish and chips and invite everyone to a
party!
    I hope Frankie's mice and my axolotl are OK and not
too much trouble.
                        ♡ from Penny

DEAR GRANDMA

Mum is helping me write this postcard because she is very sunburnt and has to stay in the shade.

Uncle Pete and Auntie Sam came to visit and we beat them at beach cricket. Penny bowled Uncle Pete for a duck and I saw a snake. And I missed a catch because I was busy surfing.

Mum is teaching me to swim and I can put my face in the water right up to my chin.

Dad is cooking his big fish tonight!
bye FRANKIE

Dear Grandma

We have been floating down the river and doing bombs off Sentinel Rock in the estuary. When we were snorkelling in the rockpool we saw seven starfish and a leafy seadragon and I drew you one. You almost can't tell they're not seaweed. I think dad has sunstroke because he dressed in seaweed and danced in front of everyone. It was so embarrassing.

A kid called James had sore feet and our friend made him sandals out of kelp! bye for now, Penny

Dear Grandma

We thought of you last night. We were watching the moon and saw shooting stars and 5 satellites and the southern Cross, the saucepan and a glow-in-the-dark crab. There were dolphins out in the waves too.

Henry says he saw weird lights in the sky AND a UFO AND a robber but you know what his imagination is like! We met a family from a country with lots of sand and no water. They had to save for 2 years just to come for a holiday at the beach.

See ya,

← Frankie

Penny

Dear Grandma, Today was the BEST day, we went diving again in the DEEP water and found SUNKEN TREASURE and SHIPWRECKS and a STINGRAY and an OCTOPUS and a GIANT CLAM!
I drew you a map so you can find the treasure if you come down to Crabby Spit. You will have to be careful because I think there will be things guarding it. And traps.
Good Luck. Love,

Henry

Cliffs
shallow
↗ To Crabby Spit
sand
Deep water
rock
X

Dear Grandma
How are your holidays going? Today mum took us
sailing and dad was worried so Frankie and I
worked the sails. We went out to an island and
saw a really dark cave which I think would have
been used by pirates! Yee hee hee and
we picked up a whole lot of rubbish in the water and a nice cup of tea!
we also found out seagulls like eating sick. It probably
has more flavour than plastic or chips. We saw 4 dolphins
and one looked right at me.
One looked a bit like
Auntie Joy.

love
from
Henry

Dear Grandma, We had a <u>real</u> adventure today!
We hired bikes and rode all around Crabby Spit.
Frankie said he saw a crocodile and I saw pelicans
and swamphens and Hannah Colman. They were
catching fish and eating them whole. YUCK!!!

And after lunch we went HORSERIDING
and now dad won't sit down. He
said his horse needed new springs.
He was being the man from Snowy
River and nearly fell into the water.
This is my invention. Do you
think I'll get rich? xxxx Penny

spring seat

I can't draw

shocks!

roll-up ladder

Hey Grandma! We have been on a ferry today to Skull Island. It is huge when you get close and smells like Henry's room because of all the bird poo. I don't think humans have ever been onto it! The sides are SO steep and there's just a little jetty.

On the pier we saw a man catch a squid. He was teasing it and it suddenly squirted a whole lot of black ink in his face! Serves him right. The man gave the squid to dad and I have a weird feeling dad thinks we're going to eat it. I'm having calamari from the shop, instead. I think I saw a giant octopus under the pier camouflaged as seaweed.

Hope you're having fun too! My hair looks like this →

love, Penny

Dear Grandma. It is so NOT good it's our last Crabby Spit
night!! We had a humungous bonfire on the beach and
people got dressed up and sang and drummed and danced.
we were HOT! ♡ Penny

Dear Grandma I have never seen such a big fire and
we toasted marshmallows. I think even some of the
grownups had a good time. It was so cool with the sea
slooshing and the music jumping. I made up a dance and
my head stayed still and my body danced around. My
dad was being funny and he's done his back.
                                    Love from Henry
DEAR GRandma I stayed up late and there was a
very big fire. I found a crab. And there were
dolphins swimming in the sea. LoVE. FRaNKiE

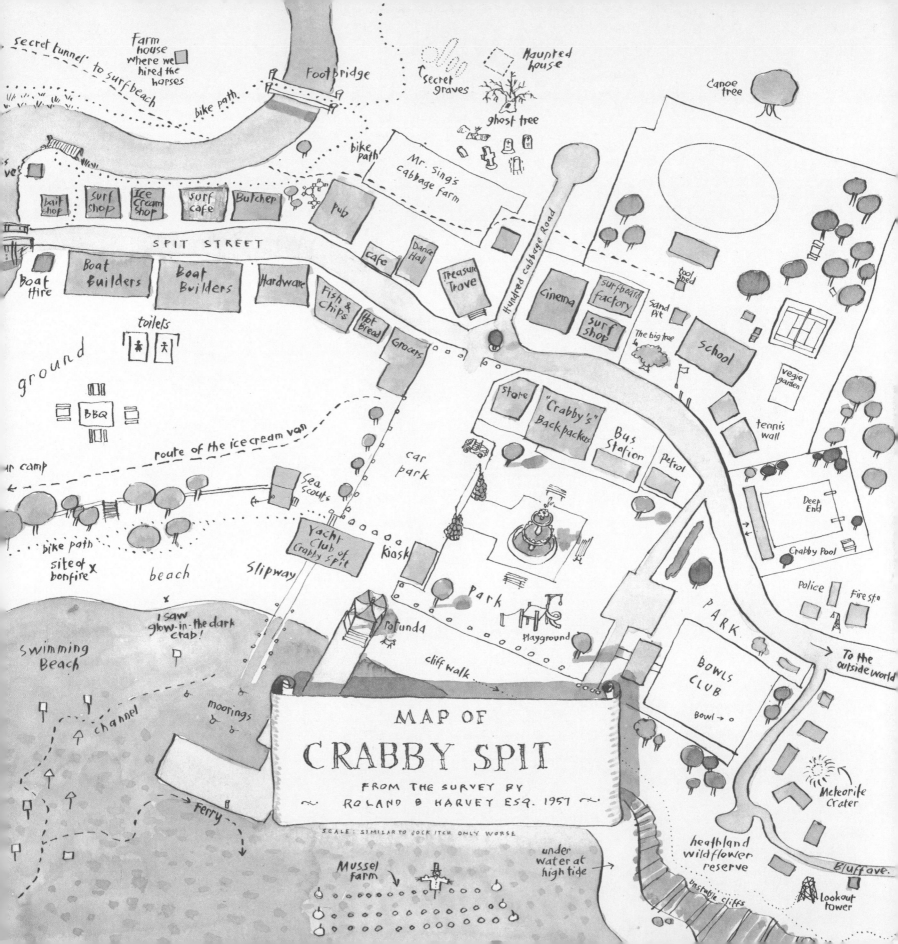

secret tunnel to surf beach

Farm house where we hired the horses

Footbridge

secret graves

Haunted house

ghost tree

Canoe tree

bike path

bike path

Mr. Sing's cabbage farm

bait shop

surf shop

Ice Cream shop

surf cafe

Butcher

pub

Hundred cabbage Road

Cinema

surfboard factory

tool shed

SPIT STREET

cafe

Dance Hall

surf shop

Sand Pit

The big tree

School

Boat Hire

Boat Builders

Boat Builders

Hardware

Fish & Chips

Hot Bread

Treasure Trove

vegie garden

ground

toilets

Grocers

Store

"Crabby's" Backpackers

Bus Station

Petrol

tennis wall

BBQ

Deep End

route of the ice cream van

car park

Crabby Pool

ur camp

Sea scouts

Police

Fire stn

bike path

Yacht Club of Crabby Spit

kiosk

Park

PARK

site of bonfire

beach

Slipway

To the outside world

Swimming Beach

I saw glow-in-the-dark crab!

Rotunda

cliff walk

Playground

BOWLS CLUB

Bowl →

channel

moorings

MAP OF

CRABBY SPIT

FROM THE SURVEY BY

ROLAND B HARVEY ESQ. 1957

Meteorite Crater

Ferry

SCALE: SIMILAR TO JOCK ITCH ONLY WORSE

heathland wildflower reserve

Bluff ave.

Mussel farm →

under water at high tide →

unstable cliffs

Lookout tower

More fantastic books from Roland Harvey

And don't miss the *Bonnie & Sam* series
created by Alison Lester and Roland Harvey